Backyard Bird Watchers

A Bird Watcher's Guide to MOURNING DOVES

By Aife Arnim

Gareth Stevens PUBLISHING

Please visit our website, www.garethstevens.com. For a free color catalog of all our high-quality books, call toll free 1-800-542-2595 or fax 1-877-542-2596.

Cataloging-in-Publication Data

Names: Arnim, Aife.
Title: A bird watcher's guide to mourning doves / Aife Arnim.
Description: New York : Gareth Stevens Publishing, 2018. | Series: Backyard bird watchers | Includes index.
Identifiers: ISBN 9781538203231 (pbk.) | ISBN 9781538203255 (library bound) | ISBN 9781538203248 (6 pack)
Subjects: LCSH: Mourning dove–Juvenile literature.
Classification: LCC QL696.C63 A76 2018 | DDC 598.6'5–dc23

First Edition

Published in 2018 by
Gareth Stevens Publishing
111 East 14th Street, Suite 349
New York, NY 10003

Designer: Laura Bowen
Editor: Therese Shea

Photo credits: Cover, p. 1 (mourning dove) rwkc/Shutterstock.com; cover, pp. 1–32 (paper texture) javarman/Shutterstock.com; cover, pp. 1–32 (footprints) pio3/Shutterstock.com; pp. 4–29 (note paper) totallyPic.com/Shutterstock.com; pp. 4–29 (photo frame, tape) mtkang/Shutterstock.com; p. 4 Mgiganteus/Wikimedia Commons; p. 5 (pigeon) Visayas/Shutterstock.com; p. 5 (white dove) Rene Bars/Shutterstock.com; p. 5 (child) spass/Shutterstock.com; pp. 7, 11 Warren Price Photography/Shutterstock.com; p. 8 BKingFoto/Shutterstock.com; p. 9 Charles Brutlag/Shutterstock.com; p. 10 B Calkins/Shutterstock.com; p. 12 Harold Stiver/Shutterstock.com; p. 13 Tobie Oosthuizen/Shutterstock.com; p. 15 Doug Lemke/Shutterstock.com; p. 16 Huaykwang/Shutterstock.com; p. 17 (top) Stubblefield Photography/Shutterstock.com; p. 17 (bottom) Crystal Alba/Shutterstock.com; p. 18 Klausrassinger/Wikimedia Commons; p. 19 Bull's-Eye Arts/Shutterstock.com; p. 21 Don Henderson/Moment Open/Getty Images; p. 23 (top) Edrich/Shutterstock.com; p. 23 (bottom) Phoo Chan/Shutterstock.com; p. 25 Factumquintus/Wikimedia Commons; p. 27 Tom Cantaffa/Shutterstock.com; p. 29 Steve Byland/Shutterstock.com.

Printed in the United States of America

CPSIA compliance information: Batch #CS17GS: For further information contact Gareth Stevens, New York, New York at 1-800-542-2595.

CONTENTS

Words in the glossary appear in **bold** type the first time they are used in the text.

MY SCIENCE JOURNAL

Welcome to my science journal! Everyone in my class is keeping a journal to help us remember important ideas that we learn. We're starting to study the **life cycle** of birds. My teacher, Mr. Garcia, told us to choose a bird to watch in our neighborhood and find out as much as we can about it and its life cycle.

I chose a bird called the mourning dove because Gramma said she sees them in the backyard. They'll be easy to watch!

Spell It Right!

mourning (not "morning") dove

The mourning dove belongs in the bird family that includes doves and pigeons.

SAD SOUNDS

Listen to Mourning Doves!

coo-OO-woo-woo-woo = male looking for a female

coo-OO-oo = male building a nest

ohr-ohr = female sitting on a nest

roo-roo = danger!

Do you know what "mourning" means? It means being sad about something. Mourning doves get their name from their sad *coo-oo* sound. They're not really sad, though. They're just making sounds, like other birds do. Their different calls and songs have different meanings—just like the different sounds we make!

I found a website with mourning dove sounds and what they mean. Hopefully, it will help me understand the mourning doves here better!

Listening to the mourning doves is like trying to learn a new language!

ALL OVER

Temperate Bird

temperate = a place that has weather that isn't too hot or too cold

Mourning doves have a fat body, small head, and pointy tail. They're light brown or tan with black spots on their wings.

Mourning doves live all over North America, from southern Canada to central Mexico. They're not afraid of people. They live in cities, towns, farm fields, and deserts. They can live everywhere except deep forests. They like to stand on bare areas of ground, but they can be spotted on telephone wires overhead, too.

RANGE MAP OF MOURNING DOVES

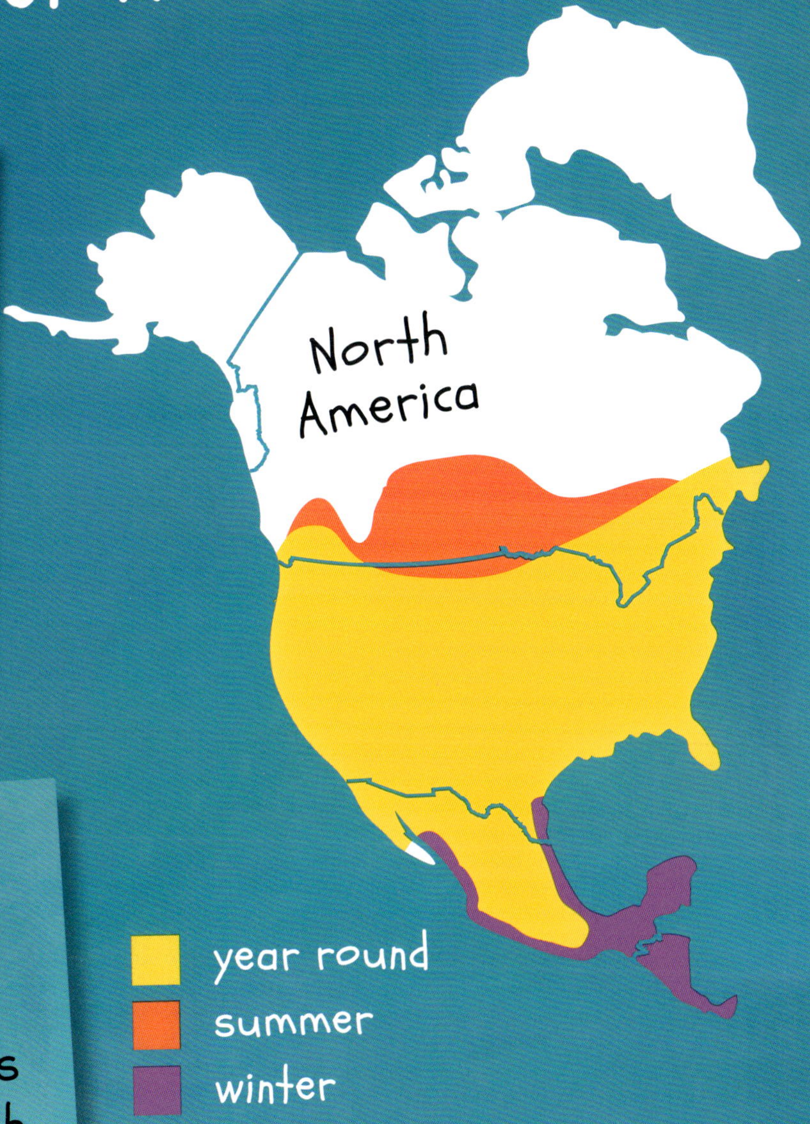

Mourning doves don't like really hot or really cold places. They like temperate areas. That's why the middle of North America is just right.

GRUB ON THE GROUND

We have bird feeders in our yard, but I see mourning doves eating under them. They like to be on the ground while they're eating seeds. The other birds at the feeder drop seeds. That's handy for the mourning doves!

Mourning doves are weird eaters. They can swallow thousands of seeds. These are stored in a body part near the throat called a crop. Then, the birds go somewhere safe to **digest** the seeds. They also eat bits of rock to help them digest. Yuck!

How Much?

One mourning dove had 17,200 bluegrass seeds in its crop!

Mourning doves eat snails and bugs, but not often!

FAST FLIERS

How Fast Is a Mourning Dove?

top flying speed = 55 miles (89 km) per hour

Mourning doves don't look very fast when they're on the ground, but they're quick in the air! They can dive, climb, and change direction suddenly. That must be helpful when they're trying to escape their predators.

Mourning doves can escape almost all their enemies, such as raccoons, certain snakes, cats, dogs, hawks, and falcons. Falcons are really dangerous because they're just as fast as mourning doves. They can knock them out of the air!

Falcons can attack a bird with their feet and then swoop down and catch it! Nasty!

LOVE DOVES?

I saw a mourning dove today flying in circles. It landed near another mourning dove. Then, it puffed out its chest, bowed, and cooed. My guess is that it's a male mourning dove looking for a **mate**. I read that's how males "show off" for females. When the male mourning dove takes off from the ground, his wings make a loud flapping noise. He wants a female to notice him.

You can also tell which doves are mates because they clean each other's feathers. That's called preening.

Go Away!

Male mourning doves chase other males from a territory after they find a mate.

Once mourning doves find a mate, they stay together through the winter. Here are the mates in my backyard!

THE NEST IS NEXT

Wow!
Some nests are so loose that you can see through them!

The mourning dove mates choose a place to build a nest. They might pick a tree, bush, or even a building. The nest might be 4 feet (1.2 m) off the ground or as high as 40 feet (12 m). That's as tall as a telephone pole!

I saw one mourning dove with a stick in its mouth. It must be the male. Males are the ones that get the **material** for the nest. The female builds the nest. The nest is flatter than some bird nests and not cup shaped.

A mourning dove nest is built near a food source. There's plenty of seed in my yard!

HIDDEN EGGS

I haven't seen the mates together in a few days, so I think the female mourning dove has laid her eggs! Females usually lay two white eggs at a time.

Both the parents take turns sitting on the eggs and keeping them warm. That's called incubation. The eggs might not **hatch** if they're cold, and it gets pretty chilly at night. The eggs will hatch in about 2 weeks, so I'll keep watching for babies!

Here is a photo of mourning dove eggs that I found in a bird magazine!

HATCHED!

I had an awesome bird-watching day! I found the mourning dove nest AND I saw the babies. I saw one of the mourning doves flying and watched it go into a tall bush. I got out my **binoculars** and saw two little heads poking up from a nest!

Mourning dove babies are called "squabs." What a funny name! The parents feed the squabs "crop milk" for the first few days. It's a liquid they make in their crop, not really milk. Then, the squabs eat seeds.

Milking It

Crop milk is also called pigeon milk. It looks like cottage cheese!

Here's a squab and its mother close up!

TRICKY BIRDS

I saw one of the mourning doves on the ground this morning. It was hopping, but one of its wings was down. I thought it was hurt. Then, another bird swooped down—a hawk! The mourning dove shot off the ground superfast!

I don't know where the birds went. However, I found out that mourning doves pretend to have a broken wing to trick birds they think are a danger to the nest. They **lure** the predator away.

Distraction!

Other birds pretend to have a broken wing, too. This **behavior** is called a nest-distraction display.

I never knew animals tricked each other. Today, I saw this bird pull off an amazing lifesaving trick!

BYE-BYE, BABIES!

Reuse and Recycle

Mourning doves may use a nest again.

I saw the squabs out of the nest today. They're about 2 weeks old. My bird book says they'll keep going back to the nest for another 1 or 2 weeks. The mother and father will keep bringing them seeds to eat until they learn to find seeds for themselves. They'll be good at flying by then.

Finally, the young mourning doves will go off by themselves to new territory. Their parents will have another **brood** I can watch!

This young mourning dove should have its adult feathers by early fall. While it's learning to fly, it's called a fledgling.

SHORT LIVES

I read that most mourning doves only live to be about 1½ years old. That isn't a long time! Some have lived a lot longer, though. One mourning dove found in Florida was 30 years old!

Sometimes mourning doves are pests to farmers because they eat grain crops. In some places, people hunt mourning doves. Luckily, these doves aren't in danger of dying out. They actually help people by spreading seeds where they go. The seeds grow into plants.

Number of Mourning Doves in the United States

350,000,000 (That's 350 million!)

Mourning doves eat the seeds of weeds, too. That's helpful for gardeners and farmers who don't want more weeds to grow.

A+ BIRD

Tomorrow, I'll hand in this journal so my teacher, Mr. Garcia, can read it. (Hi, Mr. G!) Even if I didn't have to do this for school, watching the birds was pretty cool. Now I know some behaviors to look for in other birds.

Since I've been reading about mourning doves, I've found facts about other birds that look interesting to watch. I'm going to find out what they eat and try to get them to come to my backyard, too!

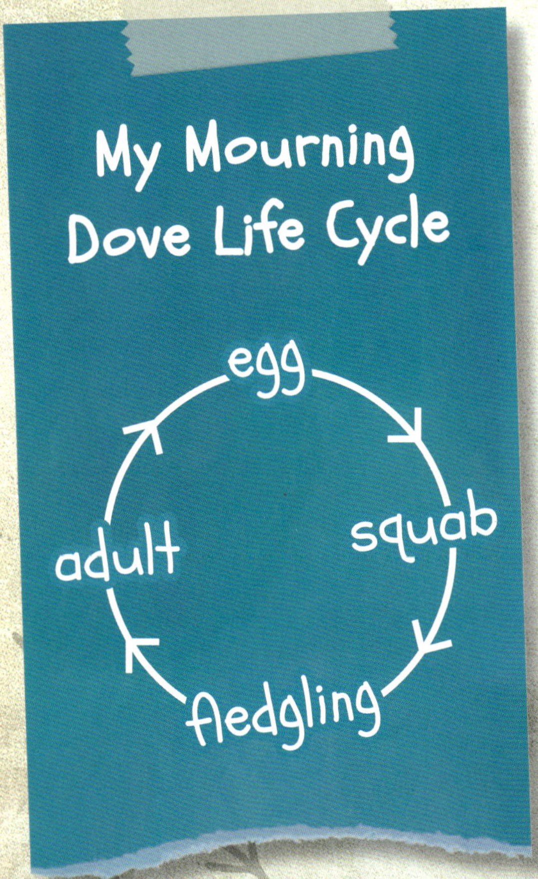

Some mourning doves **migrate**. It snows here, so my mourning doves may fly south, too!

GLOSSARY

behavior: the way an animal acts and behaves

binoculars: a tool that you hold up to your eyes and look through to see things that are far away

brood: a group of young birds that were all born at the same time

digest: to change food that has been eaten into simpler forms that can be used by the body

hatch: to come out of an egg

life cycle: the series of stages through which a living thing passes from the beginning of its life until its death

lure: to cause a person or an animal to go somewhere or to do something

mate: one of two animals that come together to make babies

material: matter from which something is made or can be made

migrate: to move to warmer or colder places for a season

FOR MORE INFORMATION

Books

Mead, Wendy. *Kids Top 10 Pet Birds*. Berkeley Heights, NJ: Enslow Elementary, 2015.

Trueit, Trudi Strain. *Birds*. New York, NY: Marshall Cavendish Benchmark, 2012.

Websites

Mourning Dove
www.allaboutbirds.org/guide/Mourning_Dove/id
Check out this great site for mourning dove sounds.

Mourning Dove
www.audubon.org/field-guide/bird/mourning-dove
Find more information about these birds and others.

Mourning Dove
www.biokids.umich.edu/critters/Zenaida_macroura/
This is a great source for learning about mourning doves' favorite seeds, so you can attract them to your yard!

Publisher's note to educators and parents: Our editors have carefully reviewed these websites to ensure that they are suitable for students. Many websites change frequently, however, and we cannot guarantee that a site's future contents will continue to meet our high standards of quality and educational value. Be advised that students should be closely supervised whenever they access the Internet.

INDEX